Inspiring Tales of Courage, Confidence, and Friendship

Emily Lin

CONTENT

INTRODUCTION

Whenever you feel sad, afraid, or discouraged;
when your dreams turn to dust . . . step back,
take a deep breath, and look within your

Affectionate

Motivated

Artistic

Zestful

Insightful

Natural

Generous

. . . self, for the strength to push through.

Trust your instincts and follow your heart.

ATTACK OF THE MANNER MONSTERS

Manners aren't just rules.
They reveal a person's true nature
and show how much someone cares.
Although it sounds simple, good manners
will open doors to great opportunities.
Most of all, good manners are the key to
building wonderful and healthy relationships.

***

Sebastian lived with his mother in a small apartment in the middle of bustling Vancouver City and, for a long time, they were fully content to be in each other's company. Sebastian loved spending time with his mother and even considered her to be his best friend. However, sometimes there was something about his attitude that wounded their wonderful relationship.

You see, although he was lively, witty, and smart, he always forgot to say nice things such as *please* or *thank you*. In fact, sometimes he purposely refused to be courteous and considerate. Unlike most kids of his age, he didn't see the value of good manners and believed that the world would stay the same without them.

"They're useless," he'd say, brushing off every trace of guilt.

As the years passed, Sebastian's dreadful habit grew worse, and he found it easier to take his horrible manners with him, everywhere he went. He casually grabbed pens and markers from his classmates in school without asking, and forcibly pushed other kids out of the way so that he could get to the front of the line at lunchtime. He never offered his seat to the elderly when the bus was crowded and , instead, he

hoisted his bag onto the seat beside him so that he could have more space to himself.

However, amidst the chewing with his mouth open, talking back, and pretending not to hear, one awful habit reigned above all the others. Sebastian took his mother for granted and never appreciated her efforts.

Every day, his poor mother came home from work, exhausted, only to be bombarded by letters from Sebastian's teachers and classmates.

"More complaints, Sebastian?" she said, reading each note. "Would it hurt to say please or thank you once in a while? You behave like a monster."

But, no matter how much she reminded him and pleaded with or even scolded him, Sebastian didn't seem to care.

Instead, he grinned, and muttered, "Manners are boring. Monsters are fun." before running off and doing whatever he pleased.

Who could have guessed that, soon, his abominable manners would get the better of him?

One Sunday morning, Sebastian's mother took him out to a nice restaurant for brunch. Excited, Sebastian couldn't wait to order. He pulled his mother over to the very first table, which had a view overlooking the plaza outside.

"We got the best table, Mom!" he said, before beginning to flip through the menu. Soon, a server took their order and then brought them delicious appetizers. In fact,

everything was going perfectly until an old couple walked in. Being the kind woman that she was, Sebastian's mother offered them their table.

Unfortunately, Sebastian didn't agree. "Hey!" he shouted. "Go get your own table! We got here first!"

"Hush, Sebastian! That's rude," his mother warned.

She turned to the old couple, smiling awkwardly as she said, "Please, have our seat. We'll be happy to take the table in the corner."

Sebastian's mother took his hand and led him to a vacant seat by the kitchen.

"But I liked it there," Sebastian whined, stomping his feet.

"Be considerate, Sebastian," his mother insisted.

Sebastian moped, and was ready to argue, but just then someone called his mother's name. It was her good friend from college. Sebastian's mother brightened up.

"Hey there! It's been so long!" his mother said, hugging her friend, before turning to Sebastien and saying, "Sebastian, say hello."

However, Sebastien was still upset about giving up their table, so he crossed his arms and huffed, before turning away.

"Excuse him. He's just upset about something," his mother apologized.

For a moment, Sebastian felt proud to get back at his mother. But after he noticed her chatting with her friend, he grew bored. He had no one to talk to and nothing to play with while they waited for the food to arrive. He was bursting with impatience, so he got up and searched for something fun to do.

While his mother wasn't looking, Sebastian skidded around the tables, bumping into the backs of customers' chairs as they ate. He stepped on a server's foot and knocked over a few plates of food, secretly enjoying his causing a commotion wherever he went. However, after he heard some complaints, he decided it was time to vanish, and he snuck into the kitchen.

Sebastian scurried past the kitchen crew, who were too busy fulfilling orders to see him slipping by. He ran into the corner, and that was when he accidentally locked himself in the chillroom.

"Oops," he said, realizing there was no way out.

Before he could call for help, the lights flickered, and then shut off. Instantly, the room grew extremely cold. Sebastien was filled with dread. He fumbled for the door handle in the darkness, muttering, "Where is it?"

He was answered by a raspy, creepy voice. "Child," it said.

Sebastian turned around, afraid of what was lurking behind him. Unfortunately, he could only see the shadows of the fruit and vegetables that were stacked on the shelves.

"Who's there?" his voice trembled.

He instantly regretted his question, when the voice replied, "I smell a boy with bad manners."

Sebastian's heart began to thump loudly, as if it were going to jump out of his chest. Beads of sweat dripped from his forehead and upper lip. If the lights would have been on, he would probably have been surprised at how pale he had turned. He pushed his back against the wall

"You don't want me," he said weakly. "Go find someone else."

But instead of being scared away, the creature chuckled, "Your foulness is delicious," it replied.

"Go away!" Sebastian yelled.

He banged his fists on the door and cried for help, hoping someone from outside would hear his cries, but no one came to his aid.

Instead, the voice snickered, “People with bad manners *are* delicious!”

Sebastien felt breathing against his ear. He shivered, as something like a deathly breeze blew against his neck. His mind froze, ad he was unable to think of any snide remark or rude gesture.

In sharp contrast his proud character, he begged, “P-please leave me alone.”

For a moment, Sebastian was certain that the evil creature would pounce on him and take him away, but instead of attacking him, the voice just started to growl, groan, and huff. Sebastian paused in disbelief,

wondering what he had done to offend the creature that hid in the darkness.

Then, suddenly, an idea struck him.

“Please?” Sebastian uttered, and he got the same reaction again.

That thing is afraid of politeness, he thought.

With all his might, he shouted, “I’m sorry for everything! I shouldn’t have been so rude. *Please* and *thank you* are such wonderful words to show how much you care and appreciate others. From now on, I promise to mind my manners and to be more sensitive to other’s feelings.”

As expected, the creature emitted an ear-shattering shriek, which caused Sebastian to cover his ears and sink to the floor. By a stroke of luck, the door to the chillroom opened just then, lighting up the room. Sebastian looked around, but found no trace of the creature. He turned and saw a member of the kitchen crew staring at him in confusion.

Sebastian took the awkward silence as his ticket to leave the scene as quickly as he could. He ran into the dining hall and found his mother frantically searching for him.

He ran into her arms, sobbing, “Mom, I’m so thankful for everything you’ve done for me! I love you so much, and I promise to be kind, courteous, and polite from now on!”

Puzzled, his mother hugged him back tightly; before stroking his hair and asking, “What’s gotten into you?”

As they ate their brunch, Sebastian told her the entire story of the incident in the chillroom. He mentioned every detail, even mimicking the creature's strange voice. His mother looked surprised, but waited patiently for him to finish.

Instead of reprimanding him, she just smiled and said, "I'm glad you've changed for the better."

And Sebastian couldn't agree more!

Sebastian realized, then, that saying *please* and *thank you* were small gestures that meant a lot. Apart from being kind words, they were a way of showing appreciation for others. He learned that showing respect didn't make him weak, uninteresting, or a lesser person. Rather, it empowered him, by securing and strengthening his relationships with others.

MESSY MIKE

Creating art and playing pretend are enjoyable moments that spark our imagination. But the deeper we delve into our games, the greater chances are that we could get carried away by the excitement. Without our knowing, we might make a mess and make others feel uncomfortable.

Although inventiveness is a great quality, we should always remember to mind our surroundings because our actions affect everyone around us.

Wherever we are and whatever we do, the simplest way to show consideration for others is to be neat and tidy.

Wonderful Ireland is home to breathtaking coastal mountains, quaint shoreline villages, and a rich history of festivals, music, and lore. It was also home to young Mike Murphy, who lived at Eight Harper Lane, with his parents.

Mike was a sweet, caring twelve-year-old with an artistic flair. He was fond of drawing, painting, and reading books that stirred his imagination. Mike was happiest during those moments when he was involved in his favorite pastimes. However, there was something about his behavior that got on people's nerves.

He was hopelessly messy!

Everyone knew about it—his parents, teachers, and friends. Even the school's bus driver complained about picking up scraps of paper filled with Mike's doodles every time the boy got off the bus. In school, Mike folded his test sheets into paper airplanes and carved pictures on his desk while listening to his teachers' lectures. During lunch time, he stacked up breadsticks and apple slices with peanut butter into food castles. He arrived home every day, yearning to create more art.

Very soon, the Murphy house had turned into an explosion of Mike's uncontrollable imagination. There were drawings on the walls, blotches of paint on the floors, and crayons stashed in the pantry. More and more, Mike's carelessness troubled his parents, who tried their best to coax him into tidying up.

"Mike, we're glad that you've got a passion for art, but this has got to stop," his mother begged.

"Creativity is one of your greatest strengths, but you also need to mind your surroundings. Some people might not be comfortable with the mess you're causing," his father added.

Mike knew things such as mixing up the laundry with newly washed clothes and leaving footprints on the sofa were wrong. Being the kind boy that he was, he tried his best to correct his behavior. For some time, his efforts were fruitful, and the house returned to a tidy state. However, it didn't take long for his imagination to overcome him again, and his clean streak only lasted for a week.

One sunny afternoon, fresh from school, Mike arrived home to a complete silence.

"Hello? Mom? Dad?" he called, setting his bag down.

He checked the living room, the backyard, and even the upstairs bathroom, but no one was to be found. He scratched his head, wondering, *where could everyone be?*

Feeling lonely, he wandered into the kitchen where he spotted a bright yellow sticky note posted on the fridge. It read . . .

Dear Mike,

We're picking up your aunt from the airport. We'll try our best to be home by 6 this evening. Hopefully, we can all go out to dinner together, if she is not too tired from the trip. Get some nice clothes ready, just in case.

Lots of love,
Mom and Dad

Mike instantly felt a wave of relief wash through him. "Thank goodness nothing bad happened," he sighed, putting the note back on the fridge.

His eyes flickered across the room, and landed on the wall clock, which struck four.

“Looks like I’ve got two hours all to myself,” he said, before sitting on a stool by the counter. “What to do, what to do?” Mike tapped his fingers on the table as his brain pulsed with creative ideas.

I could paint a picture with ketchup and mustard or make a tower out of all the pillows in the house. Better yet—I could build a humongous mud castle in the backyard!

He rummaged through the cupboards for something he could use as a shovel, until he caught himself in the dangerous act.

Nope, I shouldn’t be getting ahead of myself, he thought, putting all the items he had taken back in place. *Mom and Dad will be back soon, and I’m pretty sure they wouldn’t want to come home to a gigantic mess. I’ve got to do something that won’t turn this house into a disaster.*

He headed back into the living room, pulled a bunch of books out of his schoolbag, and spread them on the coffee table.

“Doing my homework seems like the safest option for now,” he decided, fumbling through his things for some pencils and erasers. When all his study tools were ready, Mike squatted on the floor, flipped his books open, and got to work.

“Focus, Mike, focus,” he chanted, jotting down notes in the margins.

He closed his eyes and recited his lessons, feeling proud of himself for staying put. But as soon as he reached the end of the chapter, he felt his tummy grumbling.

"Wow," he said with a hand on his stomach. "That was pretty loud."

Mike tried to ignore the rumbling sensation in his belly, but even when he pushed himself to read and write, his mind trailed off to the snacks stashed in the pantry. He leaned back and sighed, glancing at the clock which had just struck four-thirty.

"I don't think I can wait for dinner," he said, and he closed his textbook and headed into the kitchen.

Mike rummaged through the cupboards, before he saw a box of strawberry breakfast tarts in the corner. He tore the packet open and put two pieces of pastry on a heatproof plate. He climbed on a stool, popped a platter into the microwave and set the timer to one minute on medium heat. He walked around in circles while waiting for his snack to warm up, and then, suddenly, he glimpsed something red in the corner. His eyes twinkled as he looked at the new curtains his mother had sewn.

"That would make an excellent cape," he mumbled. Then, his gaze drifted to a ceramic pot with gold edging on the windowsill. "And that would make a fun crown," he added.

Mike's fingers were twitching with the excitement stirred in his bones when the microwave's bell rang, snapping him back to reality.

"My snack!" he exclaimed, taking the breakfast tarts

out. He poked at the sweet treats. "They're still a little cold, but I guess it will do," he decided.

Mike walked back into the living room and set the breakfast tarts on the coffee table. Then he squatted on a pillow and stared at his plate of food, sighing. He sat in silence, torn between his textbooks and his snack, all the while, fidgeting with the hem of his sweater.

You're doing a great job of keeping the house tidy, he convinced himself. No funny business now, Mike. All you need to do is have your little snack, then go back to studying.

He shut his eyes, hoping to regain focus—but all he could think about was dressing up and playing pretend.

Soon, he realized he couldn't contain his excitement for any longer.

"These tarts might taste better if I warm them up a little more. Then, I can eat them with some vanilla ice cream—now that'd be a real treat," he said, jumping to his feet. He grabbed the plate of breakfast tarts, sprinted into the kitchen, and put them back into the microwave. He set the timer to five minutes.

"That should do the trick!"

Mike watched as the little bulb inside flickered on. As the breakfast tarts spun inside, he turned to the windows thinking, *it's time to get crafty!*

Mike climbed onto the sink and carefully lifted the curtain rod off its brackets. Then he slid down again, avoiding the utensils on the counter. He unhooked the piece of red fabric and draped it around his shoulders, tying two ends into a knot over his chest. On tiptoes, he gently reached for the ceramic pot on the windowsill and put it on his head. Then he huddled over the table and beamed at his reflection in the toaster. *Now that's a look fit for a king,* he thought.

Mike marched around the kitchen, pretending he was entering his grand castle, surrounded by lords and knights, as the microwave hummed away. He adjusted his crown and waved to his imaginary subjects, before striding gracefully into the hallway, lifting his chin with pride. However, while he was acting out a noble figure in his own little world, he forgot about his hunger. He arrived in the living room. His eyes were twinkling in excitement as he sat on his father's recliner—which he deemed his throne—when an irresistible idea struck him.

"I know what else I can do—I can turn this entire house into my kingdom!" he exclaimed, jumping up.

Mike climbed onto the recliner's headrest and spread his arms wide.

"This will be my magnificent throne room," he shouted. "And over there can be the way to my castle's keep," he added, pointing to the stairs.

Mike leaped from the armrest and scrambled onto the sofa, huffing, "Now, all that's left is to create an opponent worthy of me and my royal army."

Trembling with excitement, he gathered every pillow he could find and stacked them up in front of the fireplace. He grabbed a large earth-toned throw blanket, glistening with golden embroideries, from the sofa and draped it over the mountain of cushions. He ran into the laundry room to fetch a couple of hangers and stuck them on each side of his monstrous creation. Then, he searched the side tables for two decorative dishes and a flashlight, which he intended to use for the creature's eyes and mouth. After putting the finishing touches to his rugged sculpture, he stepped back to admire the ferocious beast that would wreak havoc upon his imaginary kingdom—a fire-breathing dragon!

Mike ran around the room, shutting the windows and drawing the blinds closed. Then he armed himself with weapons—an umbrella for a sword, a pillow for a shield, and a spaghetti strainer for a helmet. He secured his cape around his shoulders and posed defensively before the mighty makeshift dragon, preparing to partake in the greatest battle of play pretend.

With a savage yell, Mike charged forward, He stabbed the dragon with his sword and pretended to fall back. The, he climbed onto the sofa, deciding to attack the beast from another angle. From higher ground, he thrust his weapon forward then shielded himself from the dragon's imaginary fire. Faking his fear, he rolled onto the carpet and crawled under the coffee table.

"This dragon is almost too much for us to handle," he said to his imaginary army. "We still have a chance of defeating it if we head for the keep! Fall back, now!"

Weapons in tow, Mike slithered across the carpet and crawled behind the sofa, avoiding the dragon's gaze. He signaled his make-believe soldiers, and then dashed up the stairs and ran straight for his bedroom. But before he could enter, he spotted a coat rack at the end of the hallway, which stirred his imagination even more.

Mike held out his hand, to his imaginary army behind him, and pointed to the coat rack that resembled a dark wizard looming in the darkness.

"So, it was you who set the dragon free and used it to terrorize my kingdom," he fiercely accused the wizard, drawing his umbrella as a sword. "You leave me and

my army no choice but to punish you for your evil schemes! Prepare to be vanquished, dark wizard!"

Mike roared, before getting into position. But, just as he was about to attack, a loud explosion sounded from downstairs, causing him to lose his balance. Mike jerked backwards and bumped into a side table that was filled with his mother's precious trinkets. He turned swiftly and abandoned his makeshift weapons to steady all of the decorations before they fell. He was successful and the last of them, which was a silver clock, landed in his hands.

"No," he gasped, staring at the time. It was half-past five.

Mike quickly put the clock back in place and rushed downstairs. His heart was pounding with fear, as he remembered the forgotten breakfast tarts in the microwave. He ran through the hallways, hoping that the explosion hadn't caused any damage. To his dismay, he found berry jam was splattered all over the inside the microwave. To make matters worse, a thick layer of smoke was clouding the kitchen.

Mike rushed to open the windows and the backdoor to let the foul smell out. Pinching his nose, he pulled the burnt breakfast tarts out of the microwave and tossed them into the trash bin. Then he raided the cabinets for tissues.

"You did such a good job of staying tidy by doing your homework! Why did you have to get carried away with playing pretend, Mike?" he scolded himself, as he unplugged the microwave. "Mom and Dad are going to be furious when they get home! You've only got thirty minutes

to clean up this entire mess. Plus, the living room is still a complete disaster!" he added.

Mike dampened the tissues, then scrubbed at the berry stains inside the oven.

"Think, Mike, think!" He hissed. "Use your imagination! How can you turn this sticky situation around?"

Mike polished every corner of the microwave, as he

racked his brain for ideas. Then, just as he was finishing wiping the last spot of food off, a curious thought struck him.

It was risky. However, it was a chance to redeem himself. He drew back, thinking about whether he should push through with his wild scheme. He turned to the clock, which now struck a quarter to six.

"Alright, Mike. No mistakes this time. Let's turn this house into a five-star restaurant and whip up the grandest banquet ever."

Once again, Mike rummaged through the pantry and the fridge, pulling out an assortment of mixes and seasonings as well as some bread and eggs. He dug through the cupboards for heatproof bowls, platters, and pans and set everything on the table. He made a short to-do list.

"It's go time," he said, clapping his hands.

Mike started off by making a gigantic—if slightly lopsided—omelet, stuffed with mushrooms, carrots, onions, and cheese. Then he filled some instant mac and cheese cups with hot water and let them cook. Last, he baked a batch of easy chocolate lava cakes with some flour, milk, and cocoa powder and set them in the mini oven for seven minutes. When he had finished preparing the meal, he rushed into the living room to clean up that area.

Mike dismantled the cushions from his makeshift dragon and arranged them around the coffee table. Then he dimmed the lamps, and set the mood with candles on every tabletop. He straightened out the frames and furniture but kept all of his school things out. Then he took some scrap paper, tape, and markers and transformed them into colorful crowns for his guests to wear during the dinner party. Soon, he smelled the wonderful aroma of food wafting in from the kitchen. As he followed his nose, heading into the next room, the mini oven bell rang. To his delight, he heard the sound of the lock being turned in the front door at the very moment he was pulling the lava cakes out of the oven.

That must be them, Mike thought, eyeing the clock, which now struck seven. *They're a bit late.*

He walked into the living room, fixing his hair and adjusting his cape. With a huge smile, he opened the door and greeted them, "Good evening, everyone!"

"It's great to see you, Mike! You've grown so much," his aunt said, hugging him.

"We're so sorry we're late, honey. The traffic was intense," his mother said, kissing him on the forehead.

His father eyed him from head to toe and asked, "What have you been up to, buddy?"

"You'll see! Please, come in," Mike answered, holding the door open for everyone.

He watched their expressions change from curiosity to amazement as they walked into the living room, which resembled a cozy dining room. Although the furniture and decorations weren't in proper order, the arrangement appeared quite pleasant—even stylish.

"Mike, did you do all this?" his mother asked.

"Yes, and I also made dinner!" he smiled, ushering everyone to their seats.

He adorned their heads with the paper crowns he had made earlier and handed them their napkins, before going into the kitchen to fetch the food. Slowly but surely, he made three trips back and forth, carefully carrying the main dishes, dessert, and some juice boxes on a tray. When everyone was served, he sat beside his mother and whispered, "I promise I'll put everything back in place after dinner."

She smiled and kissed him on the cheek, saying, "Thank you, dear. I'll be happy to help, too."

The family enjoyed Mike's delightful home-cooked meal while reminiscing about some great memories together. They laughed and chatted; sharing new stories, until every bit of food was eaten. After another round of juice, Mike's aunt yawned, signaling to everyone that it was time to turn in for the night.

Mike helped his father carry his aunt's bags into the guest room and hugged her goodnight before heading back to the living room to tidy up. Mike blew out all the candles as he listened to his mother cleaning in the kitchen. Then he picked up the cushions from the floor and fluffed them up before returning them to the sofas. He straightened out the carpet and the picture frames on the walls. When the job was finally done, he took off the curtain he was wearing as a cape and hung it back in the kitchen.

That night, Mike learned that creativity was his greatest strength. Being imaginative brought him joy and excitement. However, artistry on its own could result in chaos. Mike realized that pairing up his talents with tidiness saved him the trouble of causing a mess. Most of all, keeping his surroundings neat meant that everyone around him would have a good time, as well.

THE KING OF KITES

Tournaments, challenges, and games are thrilling because they push you out of your comfort zone. However, these trials are also opportunities that can help you grow. So, stay calm, give your all, and enjoy the moment. You'll be surprised by how much you can accomplish.

Festivals are the heart and soul of every culture. They are important celebrations that represent the core values of a nation and unify people from all over the country. Most festivals are deeply rooted in history, while the newer ones represent new teachings and encourage growth. Different cultures celebrate festivals unique to their own traditions, and all filled with fun and recreation. However, it's no secret that some of the biggest, most energetic, and colorful festivals are to be found in incredible India.

One of the most popular local events is *Makar Sankranti,* a celebration which marks the end of the winter solstice and the beginning of longer days. It is also the first festival of the year and is held on the fourteenth of January. The population celebrates this ancient tradition all over India in honor of the sun god, Surya, as a plea for prosperous harvests during the months ahead. Although each region of India has its own unique way of celebrating *Makar Sankranti,* every household still prepares plenty of delicious food; such as, *tilkut,* a sweet made of pounded sesame seeds and sugar; *chuda-dahi,* a healthy dish made with rice and yogurt topped with fruits; and *khichdi,* a salty porridge made with lentils, rice, and delicious spices. That dish is best served with pickle, curd, and *padpad*—thin, deep-fried flour flatbread.

What was once a local affair has now become one of the most colorful, energetic global celebrations. It attracts tourists from near and far, who all want to partake in the games, music, ancient customs and —above all —the famous kite-flying jamboree.

Seeing thousands of kites fill the sky is breathtaking, calming, and exciting all at once—and nobody is more delighted to spend hours gazing upon that spectacular scene than young Anil.

Anil lived with his parents, grandfather, and baby brother on the highest floor of an old apartment building along the coast of Gujarat. Anil loved kites, and at the curious age of six, nothing fascinated him more than the big blue world above. During the day, his imagination ran wild, wondering what lay beyond the fluffy clouds, and every night, he sat on the terrace, looking up at the stars before he went to bed.

Anil always looked forward to Makar Sankranti because he thought that flying a kite into the heavens was sort

of like touching the sky. It also thrilled him to see all the entries in the kite-making contest that was held every year at his school. All the contestants were given one week to craft the most extraordinary, eye-catching, inventive kites they could think of, and —most of all —those kites had to be able fly. For the competition, everyone gathered in the schoolyard and launched their kites into the air together. The kite-flier, whose kite soared the highest and stayed in the air the longest, was the winner and was crowned the King —or Queen —of Kites.

After months of thinking about it, Anil finally decided to enter the competition. However, he had one disadvantage —he knew nothing about making kites! Plus, it didn't help to know that the day of the competition was drawing ever nearer.

Early one morning, Anil sat on the edge of his bed, sighing as he put on his socks.

"I need to build a kite. I can't show up with nothing," he whined. Brows furrowed and back slouched, he dragged his feet across the room. He fumbled through his chest of drawers and pulled out a green shirt and an old pair of jeans, putting them on in haste. Then, he looked in the mirror and combed his hair, thinking, *What am I going to do?*

"I suppose I could always ask for help," he said to himself. "I'm sure someone in my family has made a kite before."

He tucked his shirt into his jeans, snatched up his backpack from the floor, and threw it over his shoulder.

With a skip in his step, he headed out into the hallway. As soon he reached the stairs, he spotted his father rushing up with an armful of folders and large, brown envelopes.

Anil looked up to his father. In fact, he believed his father knew everything about everything! *I bet Papa knows how to build a kite,* he thought excitedly.

"Good morning, Papa," Anil called. "Can I ask you something?"

"Good morning, my boy. What is it?" his father answered.

Anil took a deep breath while rocking back and forth on his heels.

"Well, Papa," he said, "You know *Makar Sankranti* is coming up soon, and every year, our school holds a kite-making contest. I was thinking about entering, but I have no idea how to build a kite. Do you think you can help me out?"

He eyed his father hopefully, but to his disappointment, his father shook his head and sighed.

"I'm so sorry, Anil, but I've got so much work piled up for this week. The company has scheduled me for a business trip, and I have to get lots of things prepared for when I leave the office."

His father got down on his knees and held him by the shoulders, pleading, "Anil, I hope you can understand."

"Of course, Papa," Anil answered, smiling.

“That’s my boy! I know you’ll figure something out,” his father said, ruffling his hair. “Have something to eat before going to school.”

“Alright, Papa,” Anil said and he watched his father walk into the bedroom. Then he headed downstairs, following the delicious aroma of cinnamon and buttery wheat. He went into the kitchen to find his mother hovering over the stove, stirring a pot of porridge.

"Good morning, Mama!" he greeted her, kissing her on the cheek.

"Good morning, Anil. Come have some *daliya* while it's still warm," she said.

Anil set his bag on the floor and took a seat at the far end of the table. He served himself a bowl of porridge, and then he asked, "Mamma, by any chance, do you know how to build a kite?"

"What's the kite for?" his mother asked, eyeing him curiously.

"Well, since Makar Sankranti is coming up soon, the school's going to hold another kite-making contest. I was thinking about entering the competition this year, but I've never made a kite, before."

"I see," she said, smiling. "I built a few kites when I was about your age, and I was alright at it. But you know, you should ask *Nanaji* —he's the real kite-making expert. He used to build kites of all shapes and sizes to fly with his friends. He probably still has a few tricks up his sleeve."

Anil's eyes brightened when he heard that news. He gobbled up his breakfast and washed his bowl, before looking at the clock.

"There's still some time to ask Nanaji for help," he exclaimed, running off to find his grandfather.

After looking through all of the rooms, he finally found the old man out on the terrace, watering some herbs and enjoying the sunlight.

"Good morning, Nanaji!" Anil called out, waving.

"Oh, good morning, Anil!" his grandfather replied, putting down the watering can. He noticed that Anil was grinning from ear to ear and couldn't help but add, "You look very excited today."

"I am *Nanaji!*" Anil said. "*Makar Sankranti* is coming up soon, and every year, our school holds a kite-making contest. I was thinking of entering the competition, but I've never made a kite before. Mamma told me you're an expert kite-maker, so I was hoping you could teach me how to build one."

The old man smiled and winked, whispering, "Your mother's right about that. Come on. Let's go inside and get started!"

Anil was thrilled that his grandfather had agreed to help him. In fact, *Nanaji* seemed just as excited as he was. Hand in hand, they entered the living room, chattering about how amazing their kite would be. However, as soon as they sat down to talk, Anil realized the jaw-dropping truth.

Despite his grandfather's enthusiasm, there were limits to what a man in his eighties could remember —and it really wasn't very much. Anil stared at his grandfather, who was struggling to recall the basic steps to kite-making.

"Let's see," *Nanaji* mumbled. "The first thing about kite-making is . . . Kites have tails, or was it spines—maybe both! Then there's the cover and the reel... Wait a minute. I'm losing myself. Let's start from the beginning."

Poor *Nanaji* tried his best to remember the skills he had learned during his childhood, but the more he tried to jog his memory, the more his thoughts escaped him. Anil sat beside his grandfather, while he spent five minutes going back and forth about the difference between flying lines and bridles. Eventually, Anil had to leave for school.

"Right! School! Off you go then, Anil," his grandfather said, sighing. "I'm really sorry that we went nowhere with this. My memory isn't what it used to be."

"It's not your fault, *Nanaji,*" Anil said, smiling. "I actually learned something. Now, I know the parts of a kite. Well, sort of."

Anil's grandfather smiled and pinched his cheeks. After one last goodbye, Anil rushed to join his father, who drove him to school. As the car pulled up at the school's front grounds, Anil felt more uneasy and confused than ever. He hugged his father, grabbed his bag, and got out of the car, thinking, *I guess I'll just have to make this kite myself.*

Anil walked up the front steps and headed toward his classroom. He put his bag beside his desk and played with his friends while waiting for the teacher to come in. It wasn't long before class started. Miss Devi, the kindergarten instructor, called everyone to gather on the carpet in the center of the room for an exciting lesson about the history of *Makar Sankranti.*

Although Anil enjoyed learning new things about his culture, he couldn't help but drift off in thought. His eyes darted around the room, thinking, *how am I ever going to build a kite by next week?*

In the midst of worrying, Anil turned toward Miss Devi, who had picked up a large picture book from her bag. His eyes lit up when he saw the cover page—a sea of kites in the bright blue Indian sky.

Suddenly, an idea struck him. *That's it! I know what I need to do!* he thought, fidgeting in his place. In fact, from that moment on, Anil found it challenging to sit still. He squirmed in his spot on the rug, biting his lips and playing with the hem of his shirt. His heart soared when the bell rang for recess, and to everyone's surprise, he was the first one out the door.

Instead of heading to the playground with his friends though, Anil rushed to the library, hoping he could find a book about kites. He hurried across the school, tiptoed into the library and slid past the librarian, who eyed him curiously from the counter. His jaw dropped as he stared at the humongous collection of books neatly stacked on the shelves.

"Time to get to work," he whispered.

Anil pulled out a couple of do-it-yourself kite books from the rack and squatted on the floor. He flipped through the pages, exclaiming, "Wow! There are so many shapes and sizes to choose from!"

He wanted to create something bold yet simple—most of all, it had to fly high. Eagerly, he skimmed through design after design, until a striking picture grabbed his attention.

It was a medium-sized red delta kite with tassels attached to the tips of its wings. Although the structure was fairly simple, the kite had a beautiful drawing of a sun with rays stretched across the sail.

Anil read the instructions, which he thought were easy enough for a first-time kite maker to follow.

"This is it—this is the kite! It's everything I dreamed it would be!" he squealed, only to be hushed by the librarian.

Anil mouthed, "Sorry."

He quickly returned all of the books he had taken off the shelf, except for the kite directory, which he planned to borrow. He handed the librarian the book, and she eyed him sternly as she stamped the card. Anil smiled sheepishly but he took the book, whispering, "Thank you," as he left quietly.

Now that Anil had found a solution, he felt livelier and seemed more attentive during class. When school was finally over, he ran out to find his father waiting for him by the rotunda. He hopped into the car, brimming with excitement and, as soon as he arrived home, he rushed to his bedroom. He pulled out the kite book from his bag, and got to work, thinking, *this is going to be the most amazing kite ever!*

The week seemed to pass by quickly any Anil spent each day slowly building his delta kite. He was resourceful and diligent, crafting his masterpiece with the simple materials that he found at home. He spent Monday to Wednesday designing the sail, and Thursday to Friday putting all the

pieces together. By Saturday morning, his kite was finally assembled and ready for a test flight.

Anil got up bright and early and took his kite to the terrace. He uncoiled the tether, held the handle tightly, and giddily tossed his kite into the air. He expected it to fly above the roof and soar among the clouds, but after only a split second, it fell to the ground.

"Oh, no!" Anil groaned, reeling the kite back in.

"Let's try that again," he huffed.

Once again, he threw the kite into the air, but to his dismay, it fell at his feet again.

"I don't understand! I followed all the instructions in the book. This kite should fly! What am I doing wrong?" he groaned, stomping about. He felt helpless and lost, and suddenly, he burst into tears.

At that moment, his grandfather came out onto the terrace and asked, "Is something wrong, Anil? I heard you from downstairs."

Anil sighed. "Yes, *Nanaji*. The kite-flying competition is in two days, but my kite won't fly! I don't know what to do."

His grandfather looked around.

"There isn't any trace of wind about—no wonder your kite won't fly!" the old man said.

Anil stared, speechless, as his grandfather approached him.

"Dear boy," the old man spoke, "We both know I'm old and forgetful, but if there's anything I've learned throughout my life, it's that a challenge can't be solved if you get upset over small things. I know you're determined to do well in this kite-flying contest, but sometimes, things won't turn out perfectly—and that's alright. What's important is that you keep trying until you get it right."

Anil thought for a moment, then nodded in agreement. As he rubbed his tears away, he felt a light pat on his back and looked up to see his grandfather smiling at him.

"You've got spirit, Anil. Don't worry about small failures. Come, let's keep trying."

Anil and his grandfather waited until a light breeze sprung up.

"Alright, let's give this another shot," his grandfather said.

Anil's heart pounded as he tossed the kite into the air again. He held his breath, steadying his grip on the handle. To his astonishment, the kite caught the wind and soared above the roof. However, as it continued to gain altitude, Anil grew nervous once again. He yanked the line in panic, and sent the kite spiraling down to the terrace floor.

"I suppose it was better than nothing," Anil said.

"Are you kidding? It was a terrific start," his grandfather answered. "If I can recall correctly, jerking the kite puts you off balance. You need to relax and slowly tug it from side to side," he added.

"Let's try it that way," Anil said, waiting for the breeze again, before sending the kite back into the air.

He relaxed his body and kept his gaze upward. He shifted his feet while gently tugging on the string. Before he knew it, the lines felt like an extension of his arm, and he was comfortable enough to make the kite turn—even spin!

"*Nanaji,* I think I'm ready," he beamed, turning to his grandfather, whose smile was as radiant as the sun.

Anil continued to practice throughout the weekend. Sunday flew by like a breeze. Soon, it was finally the day of the competition. On Monday morning, Anil stood among his schoolmates who were all carrying big, beautiful kites. However, even though some of their kites were larger and more colorful than his was, Anil kept his calm. He had a few new kite-flying tricks up his sleeve.

After the opening ceremony, everyone gathered out on the school grounds, and together, they all launched their kites into the air. Cheers rang out left and right, while some people groaned as their kites fell from the sky. Anil kept his sights high and focused on keeping his bright red delta kite aloft. He relaxed his shoulders, gently tugged the strings, and shifted his feet. He kept his balance even, watching

his kite soar higher and higher until it was higher than everyone else's kites.

When the competition ended, he couldn't believe that his kite was the last one flying. Shortly afterward, they crowned him the King of Kites.

Anil enjoyed the rest of the day with his family and friends and came home bearing a golden toy crown. He ran up to his room and proudly hung his kite on the wall.

This was a great day, he thought, stepping back to admire his winning creation.

Anil realized that it was important to work hard for what he wanted, and that he couldn't do his best if he was nervous or upset. Focus is just as important as perfecting a new skill. From that day on, Anil approached new challenges slowly but surely. Most of all, he learned that balance was the key to soaring to new heights.

TAISUN'S BAMBOO GARDEN

Patience always goes a long way.

In a quaint village at the heart of Southern China lived a sweet, softly spoken boy, called Taisun. He was the youngest member of the Wang family, whose household comprised his grandmother, parents, and two older brothers named Bolin and Chongkun. The boys' father worked as a farmer, like his father had before him, and their mother manned a plant shop with the help of their grandmother. They all lived in an old family home that lay on the outskirts of Hunan province, surrounded by dense forests, towering mountains, fresh air, and blue skies that stretched on until forever. It was truly a wonderful place to grow up in.

At an early age, Taisun's parents and grandparents taught Taisun and his brothers to value nature.

"We are not rulers but stewards of the earth. As caretakers of this world, it is our duty to help life flourish at all costs," his grandmother would always remind them.

One spring day, when the air was crisp with the smell of fresh earth, the boys' grandmother arrived home from the market bearing three young potted plants.

"What are those for, *Nainai*?" Bolin, Taisun's eldest brother, asked.

"These are some gifts from my friends in town," their grandmother answered. "I thought they would look lovely in our garden."

Instantly, Taisun and his brothers leaped up, begging, "Can we help you plant them, *Nainai*?"

"That would be wonderful," their grandmother replied, smiling.

They headed into the backyard and prepared their gardening tools. Then they each chose which plant to transfer into the ground.

"I'm going to grow an entire bed of lettuce, so we can enjoy fresh vegetables," Bolin announced, taking the pot with the lettuce shoots.

"I'm going to plant this peach blossom tree. It will

definitely give our garden a nice pop of color during the spring," Chongkun said, struggling to lift the sapling.

Both brothers headed to separate corners of the garden, leaving Taisun to plant the bamboo sprig that remained. It was the tiniest of the plants, amongst everything his grandmother had brought. Honestly, Taisun felt a little underwhelmed as he picked up the sprig and tapped his fingers on the pot, searching for an open spot in the garden.

"Is everything alright?" his grandmother asked, sensing his indecision.

Taisun quickly smiled and nodded. "Yes, *Nainai*. I'll care for this plant and make sure it grows well," he said, gesturing to the bamboo. Taisun took the potted plant and his tools to the edge of the garden and settled on place by a stone wall. Then he got down on his knees, dug a hole, and planted the bamboo sprig in it.

Each day, the boys ensured their plants got enough water and sunlight, and a couple of months later, they were rewarded with healthy crops.

"My lettuce is finally ready for harvesting!" Bolin cheered, earning smiles from his parents and grandparents.

"You've definitely got the farmer's gift, son," his father congratulated him, patting him on the shoulder.

"That's amazing, *Gege*," Taisun praised.

Yet, as he watched Bolin and his father harvesting the lettuce, he couldn't help but feel dissatisfied. Bolin was already proving his gardening skills, and Chongkun's tree was looking healthier than ever. Taisun's bamboo sprig had barely grown five inches, making it difficult for him to hide his concern.

He bit his lip, wondering how he could make his plant grow faster, when he suddenly felt a tap on his shoulder. He turned to see his grandmother, looking anxious.

"Is everything alright?" she asked.

Taisun didn't want to worry his grandmother. So, he nodded. "Everything's perfect, *Nainai*. I'm so happy for Bolin," he said.

Still attempting to hide his true feelings, Taisun headed quickly into the kitchen, and offered to help his mother with dinner.

That night, the family threw a lettuce-themed feast. They had steamed empress rolls, stir-fried lettuce with oyster sauce, and *san choy bow*—lettuce wraps with minced meat, water chestnuts, and hoisin sauce. They laughed and chatted during their meal until late in the evening. Then, after helping one another clean up, they retired to bed.

Taisun crawled into his bed, thinking about his bamboo plant. *One day, I'm sure it will grow big and strong,* he thought, as he fell asleep.

The next morning, Taisun and Chongkun woke up bright and early to water their plants and tended to them even more diligently as the seasons were growing colder.

Soon, winter arrived, yet the boys remained diligent throughout the chill and snow, hoping spring would come again. By March, their wishes were answered and Chongkun woke to a stunning surprise.

"My peach blossom tree has bloomed at last—and just in time for Peach Blossom Day!" Chongkun shouted, ushering his mother and grandmother outside in excitement.

"How lovely, Chongkun," his grandmother praised him.

"Your hard work has definitely paid off. We're so proud of you," his mother gushed, kissing him on the cheek.

Once again, the entire family gathered to celebrate yet another achievement. Chongkun's peach blossom tree truly was a sight to see. The family prepared tea and cakes and gathered under the shade of the fully grown tree, which was teeming with dainty pink flowers. As the family was admiring Chongkun's beautiful tree, Taisun couldn't help but feel a little empty inside. He turned to his bamboo which had only grown three feet over the winter.

One day, I'm sure it will grow bigger and stronger, he thought, rejoining his family.

Unfortunately, that day was still far away.

Taisun showered his bamboo with extra love and care, but—as the months passed—it stayed the same size. Still, he persevered and devoted himself to his plant throughout another autumn and winter. He covered the soil with a heavy layer of mulch to keep the roots warm. He also put a tent over the plant during the evenings so it wouldn't freeze. When the colder months finally ended, Taisun could no longer bear his excitement. However, within that span of time, the bamboo had only grown a few inches taller.

As the summer ended, Taisun finally lost his patience.

"I've waited three years and my bamboo hasn't even grown beyond my height!" he groaned, stomping around. "It's hopeless! I give up!"

In a raging fit, he threw his watering can down, slumped onto the ground, and begam to sob.

At that moment, his grandmother came out, asking, "Taisun? Is something wrong?"

This time, he told her the truth.

"Yes, *Nainai*. Bolin's lettuce was delicious, Chongkun's peach blossom is the most beautiful in town, but I've done nothing! I've been caring for this bamboo for three years, yet it hasn't even grown that much. How long do I have to wait?"

His grandmother waited until he had calmed down before speaking.

"Patience," she advised. "Great things always take time, and greater things need even more time. Don't stop caring for something you've worked so hard on so far. Nature does not hurry, yet everything gets accomplished in the end."

Taisun paused, letting her wise words sink in. Although he was still a little upset, he realized that things which grew too quickly often turned out to be unhealthy. He sniffled, before hugging his grandmother tightly.

"Thank you, *Nainai*," he said, picking up the watering can. "I suppose it will be worth the wait."

Taisun resumed his gardening duties, but this time, he expected nothing miraculous to happen overnight. Instead, he felt relieved to know that he wasn't doing anything wrong–all things grow and bloom at their own pace.

He spent more time outdoors, caring for his bamboo plant and occasionally whispering, "You're doing a good job. Just take your time."

With much effort, he retained the same positive attitude as another round of seasons transpired, and as the New Year approached, Taisun found that being patient wasn't difficult. Funnily enough, he felt as if he was growing alongside the bamboo—slowly but surely.

Once again, winter turned into spring, marking five years since Taisun had planted his bamboo. One morning soon after, he ran into the garden, and beamed with joy as he gazed upon a long-awaited surprise.

What was once a tiny sprig had grown into a mini colony of shoots, rising higher than the backyard walls. The plant's bark was thick and healthy, and laden with bright green leaves. The bamboo swayed gracefully in the wind and its earthy fragrance filled the air.

Taisun's heart skipped a beat and he jumped up and down, screaming, "My bamboo is fully grown!"

His family quickly gathered in the garden and congratulated him on his fruitful endeavor.

Taisun learned the value of patience, which applied to most things in life. Although the wait was long and sometimes bitter, that didn't mean that nothing was happening. Rather, it just made the reward more victorious and sweet.

Just like bamboo, all things need time to sink their roots into the soil and to gain strength, so that once they're ready, they stand tall and sturdy and continue to grow.

CHAKAN'S CHILLING ENCOUNTER

It's normal to feel afraid. In fact, everyone has their own unique fear. Yet even if there are times when we can't help but shiver and hide, we shouldn't let these experiences become limitations to how we live our lives.

We can learn to see beyond those moments that startle us or make us nervous and experience them for what they truly are, opportunities to discover that the things we find most dreadful and creepy might not be so scary after all.

Chakan woke early one summer morning, yawning and stretching as he rolled around in his bed. He rubbed his eyes, got up on his knees and crawled over toward the window, before pushing the frame open to a golden sunrise. He closed his eyes and took a deep breath, feeling the gentle breeze caress his cheeks. The wind carried the scent of jasmine in bloom and the sound of cyclists riding across the side-streets of Thailand.

Chakan smiled as he gazed at his beloved town from his bedroom window. He was excited to start the day. He got up, folded his blanket, and tucked it under his pillow. Then he crept to the door, careful not to wake his siblings. With a skip in his step, he headed downstairs, and straight into the kitchen where his mother was making breakfast.

"*Sawat dee don chao, Mae!*" he said, wishing her a good morning.

"*Sawat dee don chao,* Chakan," his mother replied, cracking some eggs into a bowl. "What are you doing up so early?"

Chakan walked over to her and hugged her from behind. "I thought I'd help you with breakfast," he said.

"My sweet son, you didn't have to wake up so early just to help me make breakfast," his mother answered, ruffling his hair.

"I know, but I wanted to," Chakan replied, smiling. "What are you cooking?"

His mother chuckled, pulling out a pan from the cupboard. “I’m making some *khai jiao*,” she said.

Chakan licked his lips, thinking about his mother’s crispy omelet seasoned with fish sauce and lime juice.

“That sounds perfect,” Chakan said.

“I’m glad you think so,” his mother commented, turning toward him. “Everything’s almost ready. However, I was thinking we could have some *pa thong ko* as well.”

Chakan’s eyes twinkled when she mentioned his favorite morning treat—Thai donuts.

"Yes, please!" he said in a heartbeat. "I've been craving them for ages. I'd be happy to go out and buy some, *Mae*."

His mother pinched his cheek. "Thanks so much for being so helpful, Chakan. Take some money from the drawer and go to the neighborhood bakery, the one at the end of the street. They always open early and serve fresh *pa thong ko* every morning."

"Right away, *Mae!* I'll be back soon!" Chakan beamed, before dashing toward the front door.

He grabbed some spare change and shoved it into his pocket. Then, he hastily put on his slippers and rushed out.

Chakan whistled as he walked down the street, squinting in the sunshine that shone on face. Soon, the summer heat kicked in, but he didn't mind even if beads of sweat were dripping down his temples—he was just happy to help his mother.

Chakan was considered a responsible child, for an eight-year-old. He was a diligent, softly spoken boy who never shied away from his chores—even if it meant having to take time away from playing games with his siblings and friends. Nothing delighted him more than seeing others smile because of his helpfulness.

Yet, despite his eagerness to help the people around him, there was something about his personality that occasionally hindered him from doing his best.

Above anything, Chakan was easily startled—and it wasn't just a phase. Everyone in his village knew he flinched,

jumped, or scurried away from the slightest disturbances at the speed of light. He was afraid of many things; such as, spiders, ghosts, or being left alone in the dark. But—most of all—he detested unfamiliar noises. Whether loud or soft, he stiffened and shivered at any sound that caught him off guard. He squealed at the cracks of lightning and hid behind his parents whenever things went *bump, rattle,* or *boom.*

These terrors usually overcame him during the night, when darkness shrouded his sight, but—little did he know—he was in for a chilling encounter that very morning, in broad daylight.

Chakan strolled by a large jasmine bush, inhaling the scent of its flowers in bloom. He sighed, relishing the morning's peacefulness. Then, he heard a strange noise that seemed to be following him.

Tap, tap, tap.

Alarmed, Chakan snapped out of his daze and swiftly turned to see what it was. To his dismay, he found the path back home empty, save for a few fallen leaves.

"Weird," he mumbled, scratching his head.

Shrugging off the odd feeling that had begun to grow in him, he spun around again and headed toward the bakery. However, before he could even cross the street, he heard the strange noise again.

"Who's there?" Chakan demanded, facing the empty sidewalk. He squinted, carefully eyeing every leaf, branch,

and pebble as he murmured, "I *know* I heard something."

He crouched down, hoping that looking at things from a different angle would help him find the source of the strange noise. Still, he saw nothing out of the ordinary.

"I'm being silly," he sighed. "I should go and buy *pa thong ko* before the shop runs out. I can't keep Mae and the rest of my family waiting for too long."

Just as he was about to give up, he caught sight of a movement in the corner of his eyes. His breath hitched when he spotted something rustling the leaves of the jasmine bush. He crept toward it as quietly as he could, wondering what lay amongst the flowers, and then he saw a pair of worn black claws peeking out from underneath the foliage.

"A monster!" he gasped, jumping to his feet. Chakan fled to the other side of the street, screaming out, "Stay away from me!"

His cheeks flushed and his heartbeat quickened. Soon, heavy beads of sweat were running down his face and into his eyes, causing his vision to blur. He halted for a moment to catch his breath when he heard the now-familiar sound of the claws tapping against the pavement—this time coupled with heavy breathing.

"No, no, no!" he groaned, breaking off into another sprint.

He screamed as he bolted past the village bakery, earning curious stares from the villagers. Although his legs grew wobbly, he refused to stop running, and he raced all the way to the end of town. He sprinted straight into the woods, and sought refuge atop a gigantic rain tree that had a magnificent crown of leaves and thick branches that touched the ground. He jumped up onto its strong bough and climbed until he was far away from the forest floor.

Supporting himself against the bark, he lifted his arms, reaching for a branch shrouded in leaves. Unfortunately, his slipper fell off, and landed in the grass below.

It's too late to head back down, he thought, hoisting himself higher.

He scrambled underneath a dense clump of foliage, pressed his back against the bark, and hugged his knees close to his chest. Then he sat in silence, hoping the mysterious creature wouldn't find his hiding place.

To his dismay, he soon heard the pitter patter of light steps treading his way. Chakan closed his eyes, listening as the creature sniffed about. Leaves crunched and pebbles clicked as it approached the rain tree, and he heard panting. Chakan held his breath, as he heard it circle the trunk. For a moment, he was sure that it would start to climb up and snatch him, and then he heard a helpless, innocent—and unexpected—cry.

At first, Chakan believed that the creature was trying to trick him into coming out of his hiding spot, but the more he listened, he more he started to second-guessing his idea.

Wait a minute. That doesn't sound like a monster, he thought, listening harder.

It wasn't long until the creature called again.

Yelp!

Its howl was followed by pained whimpering.

Yup, that definitely doesn't sound evil or dangerous, Chakan thought. *In fact, I'm pretty sure that voice belongs to something small. If anything, whatever's down there might be hurt.*

Although he was thinking a little more positively, Chakan still felt somewhat shaken after being chased around. He had not expected to experience such a chilling encounter that morning, nor was he prepared to let go of all of his fears; that was until he remembered that his family was waiting for him to bring back fresh Thai donuts.

Right, I've still got to stop by the village bakery before they run out of pa thong ko. Don't worry, Chakan, nothing bad is going to happen if you climb down this tree, he thought, giving himself a confidence boost.

"Here goes nothing," he whispered, taking a deep breath as he brushed some leaves and twigs aside.

He emerged from his hiding spot and warily peered over the edge of the branch. His gaze softened when he spotted a lonely pup lying at the foot of the tree.

"All this time, I was running away from a *soi?*" he exclaimed.

He was baffled by the sight of the tiny Thai ridgeback stray. The dog had short, silky gray fur, bat-shaped ears, and black, beady eyes that were glistening with tears. It lay on its belly, licking its paw. Chakan shifted, regarding the young ridgeback whose ears perked up at the sound of his movement. The pup looked up and met his gaze.

Dogs aren't scary at all, he thought, climbing down the tree.

He jumped down from the lowest branch, and slowly

approached the dog. He stooped to pet it. He smiled gently as the pup eased into his touch.

"There, there. Don't be afraid," Chakan said, carefully unfolding its paws.

"Oh, you've got a splinter stuck right in the middle," he added, Gently he eased the piece of wood from the puppy's pad.

Instantly, the pup's mood brightened. However, it still limped as it walked. Chakan watched as it winced every time its paw touched the ground.

"I can't leave you out here alone," Chakan said. "Not in this condition. Do you want to come home with me?" he asked the young ridgeback, before picking it up.

The pup wagged its tail and licked his nose.

"I'll take that as a *yes*," Chakan beamed. "But, before we head home, we need to stop by the bakery. I promised *Mae* that I'd buy some *pa thong ko* for breakfast."

Chakan carried the young ridgeback back to town, and stopped by the village bakery to pick up some warm Thai donuts. A few minutes later, he arrived home, excited to tell his family about his unexpected adventure.

Chakan was happy that his parents agreed to allow him to nurse the pup, until it was better. He put her in the backyard and gave her some water and food before joining his family for breakfast.

"What's the dog's name?" his sister asked the moment

he sat down beside her.

Chakan shrugged, putting a piece of *pa thong ko* on his plate.

"I don't think she has one," he answered. "She's a stray."

Chakan thought long and hard for a name that captured the pup's playful and sweet personality. It wasn't until after helping with the dishes when he finally announced, "I've got it!"

He called the young ridgeback Malee, which means jasmine in Thai—a sweet name that perfectly summed up their first encounter amongst the fragrant ivory blossoms of the plant.

With the help of his siblings, Chakan nursed Malee and played with her throughout the week. Once the pup's wound had finally healed, none of them had the heart to let her go. They begged their parents to allow them to keep the young ridgeback and promised that having the pup around would not interfere with their schoolwork or chores. Sensing that this was a wonderful opportunity for them to learn responsibility, their parents happily welcomed Malee into the family.

Chakan and his siblings were so filled with excitement and joy that they threw a party for Malee that very afternoon. They played games, ate snacks, and ran around the backyard until sunset.

By dinnertime, Chakan has discovered something important about himself.

Although it is good to be wary, he realized that actions that are solely driven by fear can lead to many missed opportunities. If it wasn't for his bravery, he might still have been hiding in the top of that tree. Worst of all, he would never have made a new friend.

Chakan learned that scary things only seemed frightening to him because he didn't understand them fully. Most of all, he learned that the best way to rid himself of fear was to face startling or daunting situations head-on.

THE TREEHOUSE CLUB

Making new friends can be challenging at first, especially when you think that they're trying to steal your other friends away. Sometimes, the fear of being left out makes you act strangely and say hurtful things that you don't actually mean.

Despite your differences from someone else, it's always great to talk things through before jumping to conclusions.

Who knows? You might end up making another fantastic friend for life!

* * *

The Treehouse Club was a top-secret group that had been founded five summers ago, in a raggedy shed atop an old oak tree in the Jameson family's backyard. It was so private that only three members belonged to the fellowship—Cory Jameson, who lived in the quaint townhouse below; and his two best friends, Jaime Delgado and Jeno Kwon. Throughout the years, the Treehouse Club kept their identity a secret from their nosy siblings, cousins, and friends at school, and they were beyond content to laugh, play, and chat among themselves.

Little did they know everything was about to change.

This year marked the club's fifth anniversary, and it thrilled the boys to celebrate another year of friendship. As they gathered in the treehouse to plan for the big event, they heard the noise of a low-pitched car engine in the distance, accompanied by the sound of screeching wheels. The boys huddled curiously around the window of the treehouse. They spotted a large moving-van approaching quickly, with a small blue car tailing behind it. To their surprise, the two vehicles parked in front of the house right across the street.

Cory and his friends watched as two men jumped down from the van. They opened the trailer and began hoisting large pieces of furniture onto the lawn. Soon, a middle-aged woman emerged from the small, blue car, followed by a pale, skinny boy with bright orange hair and a face full of freckles. He had innocent eyes, looked fairly quiet, and seemed quite tall for his age.

"I guess those are your new neighbors, Cory," Jaime whispered.

Cory, Jaime, and Jeno stared at the people next door—who had their backs turned against the treehouse—for some time. The club's members could have remained undercover if it had not been for Jeno's huge sneeze, which caused the red-haired boy to spin around and meet their gaze. Instantly, the nosy members of the Treehouse Club ducked, in panic, and retreated into their shed.

"Oh, no! We've been caught!" Cory hissed, cupping his cheeks.

"I'm so sorry, guys! Maybe the new kid will forget we're here if we stay super quiet," Jeno whispered, his hands trembling.

Jaime found a small hole in the wall and peeped through it. His eyes turned as round as the moon when he announced, "Code red, code red! The stranger is approaching our headquarters! I repeat, our secrecy has been compromised!"

The club members shut their eyes and held their breath, afraid of being discovered.

Luckily, the boy's mother called to him for help. "Dean! Come inside and bring those boxes for me, please," she said beckoning towards the lawn.

Jaime peeped through the hole in the wall and watched the new boy pick up a couple of cardboard cases, walk up the front steps, and then shut the door with his heels.

"Oh, good! He's gone," Jaime said, fanning himself.

Cory, Jaime, and Jeno sighed in relief.

"That was close," Cory said. "Guys, we can't afford to let anyone know about our secret club, especially a stranger."

"Well, we know his name is Dean," Jeno pointed out naively, earning stares around the room.

"Knowing his name doesn't mean we actually know what kind of person he is," Cory answered, quickly glancing over at the window.

"You're right," Jeno nodded.

At that moment, Cory's father called, "Hey there, boys! Jeno and Jaime's parents are here to pick them up. Come down as quickly as you can."

"Alright, Dad," Cory answered.

"I guess that's all for today, guys," he added, turning to his friends.

"Don't worry. We'll see each other again on Monday. Have a great weekend, guys," Jaime said, climbing down the tree.

"Aren't you coming down, Cory?" Jeno asked.

"I think I'll stay here for a bit and keep a lookout," Cory replied.

"Cool! Tell us next week what you find out," Jeno said, heading out.

Cory waved goodbye and then went back to peeping through the tiny hole in the wall. He watched as the boy and his mother moved boxes into their new house. Cory couldn't quite put his finger on it, but there was something about Dean that he wasn't comfortable with.

Maybe it's because he caught us spying on him, Cory wondered.

Soon, it grew dark, and Cory's mother called him for dinner.

"I guess that's all I have to report to the guys," he muttered, climbing down the tree.

Although nothing bad had happened, Cory couldn't help but feel worried. He spent the entire weekend trying to learn all that he could about the new kid next door. When Monday finally arrived, Cory ran into class, excited to see his friends again. Instead, he saw his red-haired, freckle-faced neighbor sitting in the front row.

Cory stiffened; his feet glued to the floor.

“Hey, isn’t that the new kid, Dean?” whispered Jaime, coming up from behind.

Cory nodded.

Soon, Jeno entered the room. His bright smile faltered once he realized who his new seatmate was going to be.

“Guys, the new kid took the spot beside me. What do I say if he suspects we were spying on him?” Jeno’s voice trembled.

“Just change the subject,” Jaime suggested.

“And whatever happens, do not mention our club,” Cory warned.

“But—,” Jeno started, only to be cut off by their teacher, Miss Minsky.

“Good morning, everyone! Please settle down,” she said.

Cory and Jaime took their seats in the back row, staring at Jeno, who reluctantly sat down beside the new kid.

“Before we begin, I’d like everyone to welcome our new student, Dean Rivers,” Miss Minsky announced after shuffling some papers on her desk.

“Hi, Dean,” the class greeted the boy in a chorus.

"Hi," Dean mumbled back sheepishly.

"Dean just moved into town last week and is going to be joining us for history and math," Miss Minsky said. She turned to Dean, adding, "Don't be afraid to reach out to me or any of your classmates if you need anything."

When the introduction was through, Miss Minsky faced the class again.

"Let's begin with a review of last week's lesson. Please pass around this short worksheet. To make things lighter, we can all pair up with our seatmates."

She eyed Jeno, saying, "Why don't you and Dean partner up for this activity?"

Jeno gulped as he received the worksheet, and then he turned to his seatmate.

Cory and Jaime watched Jeno from behind, while the class was busy with the exercise, and were surprised to see that he was smiling. They couldn't wait to hear what he had to say about Dean, when the bell rang for recess.

"How was it?" Jaime asked, pulling Jeno close.

"Dean's actually not that bad," Jeno said. "I'm going to show him around school. Do you guys want to come?"

Jaime also seemed interested in befriending Dean, but before he could agree, Cory butted in with a snide remark.

"No thanks, Jeno. Jaime and I are going to plan our

club's anniversary party. You can join us when you're done playing around with your new friend."

Jeno nodded and pursed his lips. "Alright, then. I guess I'll see you guys later," he said, heading off after Dean.

Cory pulled Jaime into the library, and together they came up with some games, snacks, and fun activities for the big day. However, even if thought they were having fun sharing their ideas, both boys sensed some tension in the air.

Jaime didn't like brushing Jeno off and Cory felt betrayed. He hadn't realized— that deep down—he was afraid of losing his friends. Cory knew that ignoring Dean was rude, but instead of being thoughtful, he distanced himself from Dean even more. He frowned whenever Dean passed by and rolled his eyes whenever Jeno talked about him. To make matters worse, Jaime seemed to warm up to the new kid. Soon, Jeno and Jaime started spending more time with Dean and less time hanging out in the treehouse.

"Dean this and Dean that," Cory grumbled to himself, when no one was around.

Still he put a lot of effort into taming his temper, only to have it escalate again later that week.

Hungry and tired, Cory had always looked forward to having lunch with his friends in the cafeteria and so he was flabbergasted to find Jaime and Jeno sitting with Dean at their special table. Jaime and Jeno smiled, and called out him to join them. Instead, Cory said, "playground after school," before storming off, too angry to notice how embarrassed Dean looked.

When the last bell rang, Cory headed to the park across the street, furious with his friends who arrived a few minutes later.

"Hey, why are you acting so weirdly?" Jaime asked.

"Is something wrong? You can tell us," Jeno added.

"Don't pretend you don't know what's going on," Cory accused them. "You've been spending so much time with Dean that you've forgotten our club's anniversary is coming up!"

"About that," Jaime said. "We actually wanted to ask if we could invite Dean to our celebration. He's actually a really great guy."

"What? You told him about our club?" Cory gasped.

"Nope. He figured it out by himself," Jeno answered. "Turns out that he was in a secret club with his friends back in his hometown. Isn't that cool?"

"You know, Cory, maybe we should give him a chance. He's new in the neighborhood and far from everyone he knows. He's pretty lonely," Jaime pointed out.

"It doesn't matter," Cory hissed. "The Treehouse Club is private for a reason. We can't start letting strangers in."

"Well, maybe we should reconsider. Change can be good sometimes," Jaime sighed.

Unfortunately, Cory was too angry to see sense. “The Treehouse Club is for *official* members only—and there isn’t any room for newcomers,” he yelled, only to be met with awkward looks from his friends.

The boys stood in silence as the other children played around them. It wasn’t until the school bus arrived that Jaime finally found the courage to speak.

“Our club is special, Cory, but that doesn’t mean we can’t make new friends,” he said, turning away.

“Sorry, Cory,” Jeno added, following Jaime.

Cory was left alone, feeling miserable. He masked his hurt by muttering, “I don’t need those guys,” and he marched home alone.

He arrived to an empty house. Seeing that his parents weren't home from work yet, he screamed as loudly as he could. Then he threw his bag on the couch and kicked his shoes into the fireplace, hoping it would make him feel better. When that wasn't enough, he headed into the backyard and took refuge in the treehouse.

Cory crawled into the hut, struggling to take his mind off his friends, but instead of finding peace, he just felt longing, aching in his heart.

"I'm kidding myself," he said eventually, glancing around the shabby room that was filled with wonderful memories of fun times with Jaime and Jeno.

Soon, tears clouded his vision, and in a raging fit, he stomped his foot hard on the wooden floor. To his dismay, one floorboard broke loose, and his leg shot right through the tight hole between the boards.

"Help! I'm stuck!" he screamed, wiggling his leg.

He was beginning to think that he would never break free, and just when he was about to lose hope, he heard footsteps approaching.

"Mom? Dad? Is that you?" he called, turning toward the doorway.

It was not his parents. Instead, he found himself staring at an unexpected visitor.

"No, it's just me," Dean announced. "I heard someone screaming, from across the street, and figured they were in trouble. Would you like some help?"

"That'd be nice," Cory mumbled shame-facedly.

Dean crawled behind Cory, wrapped his arms around his chest, and pulled. Still, Cory didn't budge.

"Huh, you seem pretty stuck," Dean said, scratching his head. "Let's try breaking the floor open a little more, then maybe your leg can pass back through."

"Sure," Cory answered.

The two boys joined forces and tugged on a loose floorboard. The stubborn plank of wood snapped off easily enough, leaving more than enough room for Cory to pull his leg out of the hole. He yanked his foot up and tumbled over backwards. He hugged his knees close to his chest and, for the first time, had an actual conversation with Dean.

"I'm sorry I was cold to you. It's just that nobody ever came between me and my friends before, and I was afraid you'd steal them from me," he admitted.

Dean shook his head, saying, "I could never steal your friends from you. In fact, all we've been talking about is how much fun you are to be around. You've got great friends, Cory, and they've got you, too. You guys are super lucky to have each other."

At that moment, Cory heard his parents' car pulling up in the driveway.

"I had no idea. Again, I'm really sorry," Cory mumbled. "Hey, would you like to stay for dinner and fill me in on everything I missed out on with you and the guys this week?"

Dean agreed in a heartbeat.

"That'd be great! But first, can I borrow your phone?" he asked. "I just need to tell my mom where I am."

Cory's parents were delighted to have Dean visit for dinner, and he ended up staying longer than expected. The boys chatted and played, and discovered that they had a lot in common.

The next day, they carpooled to school. Jeno and Jaime couldn't have been happier to see the two boys walk into class together.

“Guys, club meeting,” Cory said.

Cory, Jaime, and Jeno huddled in the corner of the room as Dean watched from the doorway in puzzlement. After a while, the three boys approached their new friend, grinning from ear to ear before breaking some amazing news.

“Dean, we’d like you to join our secret society—the Treehouse Club!” they exclaimed.

Barely holding back his tears, Dean nodded and said, “Yes, please!”

When the first bell rang and everyone headed to their seats, Cory recalled what had happened over the past week. He realized it wasn't right to judge people, before getting to know them. Moreover, it had been silly to think a stranger could rip his friendships apart.

Now, he knew that friends came in all shapes and sizes, and showed up during different times in one's life. Most of all, whether they were old or new friends, Cory realized that each one was special and deserved to be listened to, respected, and accepted for who they were.

CONCLUSION

We all go through happy and sad times every day. However, bad experiences shouldn't stop us from being **kind, generous,** and **courteous.**

No matter who we are, or where we come from, we can always spare a moment to **listen** to others and to **lend a helping hand** to anyone who crosses our path.

Let's aim to be the best we can be and make these moments last.

Made in the USA
Middletown, DE
31 August 2024